WHAT DOES GOD WANT ME TO DO
RIGHT
NOW

Ten Simple Rules
For a Passport to Heaven

HELEN GLOWACKI

Novels by Helen Gumienny Glowacki

When God Broke Grandma's Heart
When God Took Grandma Home
When Grandma Chased the Spirits
The Granddaughter and the Monkey Swing
The Story of God's Plan of Salvation
Abiding Faith, Hidden Treasure
And Then They Asked God
Celeb's Testimony

Why God Why Series by Helen Glowacki

To What Purpose?
Why God Why?
Why Trust Scripture?
Life after Death And The Coming Tribulation
What Does God Want Me To Do Right Now?
Do Our Little Sins Really Count?
What Do Angels Do?

Other non-fiction Books by Helen Glowacki

Politically Incorrect: The Get Some Gumption
Handbook When Enough is Enough
What No One Is Telling You about Addictions
How to be Happy

* * * * * * * * * * * * * * * * * *

Authors Website: www.helenglowacki.com
Face book: http://www.facebook.com/pages/The-Grandmother-Series/155300907853909?ref=ts

WHAT DOES GOD WANT ME TO DO
RIGHT
NOW

Ten Simple Rules
For a Passport to Heaven

HELEN GLOWACKI

This book was printed in the United States of America

The King James Version (KJV) of the Bible, which is
public domain in the United States of America, is used
for all scriptural references throughout this book. The
application of which is based upon the opinion,
research and religious belief of the author.

Cover assembly by: Darren Robinson, dr design &
Associates.

Website by Daniel Patrick Landolfi

To order additional copies of this book visit
www.helenglowacki.com

For more information email helen@helenglowacki.com

MISSION STATEMENT

To Serve

God

With All Our Strength

And

All Our Heart

HELEN GLOWACKI

ACKNOWLEDGEMENTS

Very special love to my husband Wally who provides so much support to my work, makes my computer behave and makes my world secure. Thanks to my children and grandchildren for the constancy of their love and encouragement. Special thanks to Danny Landolfi for his incredible help and for the design and maintenance of my website. Thanks to Darren Robinson for assembling the covers for my books, to Matthew Burniston, Colette van Loggerenberg, and Raphael Wyngaart for promoting my books in England and South Africa respectively and to Kathi Leipp who works in Germany to promote my work and to translate my work into the German language. Thanks to the wonderful people behind the scenes who help distribute and donate my books to substance abuse and cancer centers, mission schools, and prisons around the world, and through this distribution help find that last soul God seeks. Thanks to Rev. Kevin Speranza and Rev. Herold Ambroise for their prayers and assistance. Thanks to Richard Levinson for providing the first opportunity through which I could develop this work. Thanks to my brothers and sisters and ministers in faith who so freely give their love and their prayers to me, and to my Face book friends who also pray for me and also support this ministry. But most of all, we thank our Heavenly Father for His inspiration, guiding hand, protection, and never-ending love. May this work bring joy to His heart and help find that last soul! Thank You!

NOTE TO THE READER

The non-fiction books by Helen Glowacki represent the opinion, research, religious beliefs and scriptural interpretations of the author and are not meant to be used in lieu of the advice of ministerial, theological, medical or psychological experts.

The novels by Helen Glowacki are works of fiction. References to real people, events, organizations, or locales are intended only to provide a sense of authenticity, and are used fictitiously. Characters, incidents and dialogue are drawn from the author's imagination and are not to be construed as real. Any resemblance to actual persons, living or dead is entirely coincidental.

No part of these books may be used or reproduced in any manner whatsoever without written permission except in the case of brief quotations embodied in critical articles and reviews.

The King James Version (KJV) of the Bible, which is public domain in the United States, is used throughout the books by this author.

For further study, the author recommends the New King James Version (NKJV) of the Bible as easier reading and less usage of the old world language while remaining true to the original text.

"One thing have I desired

of the Lord,

that I will seek after;

that I may dwell

in the house of the Lord

all the days of my life,

to behold the beauty of the Lord,

and to enquire in his temple."

Psalm 27: 4

MESSAGE FROM THE AUTHOR

Sadly, many people think about, and even wish for a closer relationship with God but feel that it is too time consuming to pursue. They are curious about what it takes for one to find faith yet are hampered by their mistaken belief that there are too many pre-requisites; too many rules to follow. Some perceive faith to be a great mystery which is not available to everyone and others believe that they would have to sacrifice the more imminent commitments which their lifestyle demands. Sadly, there are also some who believe that their sins, especially those they believe they may continue to commit, cannot under those circumstances, be forgiven.

This attitude is understandable given the busy harried world in which we live where we *are* bogged down by so many diverse events and responsibilities and where few know what scripture tells us. When one rarely finds time to relax, one might wonder how they could ever give time to

God. This lack of knowledge is also understandable when one considers the power of evil. It is very difficult to rebuke temptation without knowing why we are tempted, and when we do not possess the tools to overcome those temptations.

But in reality, just a *little* knowledge about what God really asks of us goes a long way toward dispelling the myths and misconceptions about God and can bring us into the wonder of a true relationship with Him. In fact, learning that God can and does help us meet our daily responsibilities when we offer our heart to Him is usually an amazing revelation. Learning that God understands why we sin and that He gladly forgives the contrite heart can also help many make the decision to begin to seek God and develop their faith. Acquiring faith can be as simple as making the decision to do so.

God is fully aware of what we go through and of every constraint which life places on us. He is also aware of the shortcomings we have. He understands that in many cases our shortcomings are inherited, and thereby deeply instilled in our psyche. God does not demand perfection of us. He simply wants us to desire, to strive, to *want* to become all that He looks for. It is our *heart's attitude* toward God that counts, and the *sincerity* with which we approach Him. Since He can look into the heart of every man, we can never fool God. We can never *pretend* to a sincere, or contrite, or striving heart because He already knows *everything* about us.

But if we come before God with the right heart's attitude, explaining our concerns and asking Him to show us what we can and must do, He will help us on our journey to faith. He will help us learn about the incredible plan He has laid out for mankind and why He has done so. We will learn that God offers us a love which today's world cannot offer. And once we are touched by that love, we long to be a part of it and desire to learn how we too can love in that manner. What many don't realize however, is that we have an enemy who does not want us to take that first step toward building a relationship with God. His goal is to keep mankind separated from God.

Sadly, if we continue to slough off all matters pertaining to our spiritual life, and ignore the many times when God knocks at our heart's door with an invitation, we will find ourselves bereft of the gifts He wants to give us here on earth and in eternity. We may even find ourselves bound with the enemy of man and God, and in torment for all eternity.

God gives *everyone* the opportunity to accept His offer of love and grace, and He offers it in many forms and in ways that can appeal to every soul. He has given *all* men the free will to give their yes word to Him....or not. He wants *all* men to be saved from the damnation which sin will bring them, yet many will spurn that offer. Some spurn God's offer out of ignorance, some because Satan blinds them to the truth and sadly, some because they simply want to wait until their life becomes less hectic. All these excuses are the result of the work of Satan who *must* prevent man from accepting what God offers.

Part of our understanding about God's plan is the revelation of who Satan is, why He has power over mankind, and what his goal is. As we learn of God's plan of salvation, we also learn how God is working to create a new world which will be free of satanic influence and therefore free of all evil and all unrighteousness. Thus God's offer of a new world is also an offer for a future which will be free of all sorrow and all tears.

I have written this book to help explain God's plan of salvation and what it means to all of us. In ten chapters it will provide the steps for obtaining what I term our passport to heaven. Just as we might need a passport to leave this country to travel to another country, there are certain requirements for leaving this earth and all its unrighteousness to live forever in God's new and perfect and righteous kingdom. And just as each of us would want a kind, loving, empathic spouse for our child, so does God seek a kind, loving and empathetic people for His kingdom.

We cannot however, develop the level of love God seeks if we never experience love in its purest form. Pure love produces the desire to care about others and to express and receive a stedfast love. Pure love is a love which our world does not now possess, but which God freely extends to us. The love which we as humans know can be fickle and conditional, whereas the love God has for us is eternal and unconditional and offers us the ability to free ourselves from the power of evil.

While all this might appear to be complicated, it really is very simple, and the following pages will explain why. Once we learn where sin comes from, why we must experience evil, and what God wants to bring out of our experiences, we begin to understand the loving plan of salvation which God has put into place for those who will accept His offer. Once we open our heart to God, we change; we grow in love and compassion and we learn the value of using our free will to make the most important choice we can make in our life: to choose between good and evil.

To fully understand God's plan for mankind it will be important to keep an open mind as we discuss what transpired in heaven before Adam was created, what role Satan plays in our lives, and why Satan must keep man away from God. What may make these facts difficult to accept is that our world has recently been filled, through books, movies, comics and television shows, with supernatural stories featuring good and evil action figures, satanic influences, occult practices, zombies and werewolves, to name a few. The manner in which these are portrayed cause us to believe that an evil power only exists in a fantasy world and is thus to be scoffed at otherwise. This perception has not occurred by accident but has been planned and executed by Satan for the specific purpose of making us uncomfortable with any serious discussion about devils and spirits and the powers they might wield over mankind.

By "scaring us off" discussions about what scripture tells us regarding satanic activity, Satan succeeds in making us avoid the subject of how and why evil works in our lives, and why it is necessary for him to cause us to become complacent about God. Satan's goal is to prevent mankind from believing God's plan *and* ignorant of what Satan can do to accomplish that goal.

With this in mind, I therefore ask you, the reader, not to negate what you will read in the following pages as simply an unbelievable supernatural fable, but to open your heart to the entire explanation. This will allow you to gain a complete understanding of God's plan of salvation. As these truths unfold, and the beauty of God's gift to us and

His offer for our future is understood, you will also learn about life after death, how far grace reaches, and why entering the new heaven and earth requires the complete absence of evil.

Parts of this book will simply provide the chapter and verse where you can find the supporting scripture. Other parts will contain the entire quotation. My goal is to provide the reader with the ability to further research what is written here, yet allow the information to be presented in an easy to read, easy to understand manner. I hope to demonstrate what we are to do, why we are engaged in a spiritual war, the outcome of that war, and what God's goal is for us as we move through life.

I recommend that before embarking on the project of reading this book, that you pray and ask God to open your heart, open your understanding, and lead you to His truths. If you complete this book and continue to doubt, keep praying that God will give you what you need so that in time, your heart can be touched by the magnitude of His offer. Ask Him to secure your future and allow you to experience the incredible love He has for you.

This book, *"What Does God Want Me To Do Right Now?* is the fifth book in the Why God Why series. Each book is intended to explain, in simple language, what scripture tells us about the plan God has for mankind and how we can move through our life under God's blessing. The title of each book portrays what information is covered in that particular book.

I hope you enjoy what you read and will then be willing to share what you have learned with others. May God bless you and keep you always, may He open your understanding of His words, and of His plan for your life, and may you be drawn ever closer to His heart.

Helen Glowacki

TABLE OF CONTENTS

****

Chapter 1:

Chapter 2:

Chapter 3:

Chapter 4:

Chapter 5:

Chapter 6:

Chapter One

CHARLIE

Years ago, the world was very different. We didn't lock our doors and we knew our neighbors. We lived in a world where trust was easily given, where love for our fellowman thrived, and where integrity was our greatest personal asset. But as the information age descended upon us and a desire for more material possessions claimed our energy, life changed and we became envious, we lost the ability to love one another, and to keep our word. Growing up in that slower paced and more charitable world encouraged us to practice our faith, and to seek a close relationship with God. We looked to God as the instructor who would teach us how to live our life. We accepted that heaven was the reward we would receive for living as God asked us to live.

But then we began to feel the pressures of credit card debt, broken relationships, job competition, blatant dishonesty, and a corrupt government going unpunished. We began to lose our easy trust and our ability to love. We began to compromise our once staunch level of integrity. We no longer had the time or energy for the conversations we once held with our parents and children and grandchildren about the importance of a good character and the joy of godly pursuits. We no longer had conversations about our experiences of faith or about a bible study which increased our understanding, or about how to forgive or how we could help our neighbor. Thus we lost the gift of learning from these conversations. As a result we now have a generation of people whose parents and grandparents may never have spoken of their faith, of their experiences, of those things which brought them closer to God. Yet, despite these failures, many still seek God and feel a hunger in their heart for righteousness even though they do not know how to satisfy that hunger.

Many years ago I spoke with an elderly gentleman who grew up in that earlier time when a handshake was more binding than a contract. He would often talk about the guardian angel God has sent to look after him. He had named this angel "Charlie" and said that he spoke to Charlie every day. He would ask Charlie to stay by his side and help him act in ways which were pleasing to God and to help him keep his family safe. Though this gentleman had not been brought to church as a child, when he had children of his own, he and his wife made the decision to attend church services every Sunday and to provide their children with a religious education.

The church they attended taught them what God required of them and the importance of living one's life in accordance with Biblical principles. It also taught them to trust God when life brought them difficult circumstances. They were assured that if they did their best to live in this manner, were sincerely sorry for their sins, and asked God to forgive them when partaking of Holy Communion, God would look after them and they would go to heaven. This gentleman's faith was simple and unwavering, and I am sure that it was pleasing to God, despite his not knowing every nuance of God's plan of salvation. His faith kept him close to God and believing in the salvation God offered him. What was evident when listening to this god-fearing man was that God *does* look into one's heart and if He finds a child-like faith, He does not require an in-depth understanding of His plan for mankind. It seemed clear that when this man' faith began to form, the circumstances in which he lived did not bombard him with the hectic pace of life we now experience. He was not subjected to the information age in which we are currently steeped, nor the time constraints, stress, doubt, and false doctrines which work in today's world to make us question the existence of God and destroy our faith.

In today's world, many may desire to nurture their faith, and believe that there is a God, but are unable to find their way through the maze of false information, nor work through the ridicule aimed at believing in God and trusting that scripture is the word of God. Sadly, because today's population is mostly well informed, even arrogant about their level of knowledge, and they labour under severe time constraints and financial pressures, they have, out of necessity, learned to exercise caution. Their trust has been damaged by false information, untrustworthy people and even by thinking that they already have all the answers. Therefore they seek a greater understanding....and empirical proof.... of what they are asked to believe. Adding to this dilemma, in many circles people scoff at scripture and proclaim it to be inaccurate, even mythical. In fact, one of the mini-books I have previously written (which is similar in size and style to this one) is titled *"Why Trust Scripture"* and explains why we *can* trust scripture and how scripture even correlates carbon dating with the Creation. I chose that subject to negate the many claims that we cannot trust scripture and thereby cannot trust that scripture is the irrefutable word of God.

But the bottom line is that if we desire to find faith and to please God, we must put forth the effort to learn about God. If this effort takes us on a journey through the supernatural, so be it. If we commit to the journey and explore what God tells us, then we can make an *educated* decision about whether or not to accept what we have learned. At the very least this will offer God an honest effort rather than a closed mind. Sadly, it is the closed mind which ends such a journey and which greatly interferes with our quest for the truth. We can no longer learn once we close our heart *and* mind to what we are being told. In fact, scripture tells us that as God's plan reaches fruition there will be a great falling away of faith. (2 Thessalonians 2:3). Since evil can influence the mind and inhibit our ability to comprehend God's majesty and providence, we need to employ our heart along with our mind to believe what the mind alone cannot or will not comprehend. Scripture tells us that Satan can blind the minds of men to the word of God (2 Corinthians 4:4). Scripture also tells us that God desires to open our heart. Sadly it is often the arrogance of our mind and the false pride of personal intellect which holds us back, closes our heart and robs us of the many gifts which God wants to give us.

Scripture provides us with a warning about the loss of faith and the denial of God's truths which we now see occurring in the world, and tells us in 2 Timothy 3:1-7: *"...in the last days, perilous times shall come. For men shall be lovers of their own selves, covetous, boasters, proud, blasphemers, disobedient to parents, unthankful, unholy, Without natural affection, trucebreakers, false accusers,* *incontinent, fierce, despisers of those that are good. Traitors, heady, high minded, lovers of pleasures more than lovers of god. Having a form of godliness but denying the power thereof...**ever learning and never able to come to the knowledge of the truth.***"

Thus the remaining nine chapters of this book will attempt to explain what scripture tells us about God's plan of salvation. It will attempt to describe those things which we must do to become those whom God is grooming for the new kingdom he will create. It will explain who works to thwart that plan and why. It will address life after death, grace, and why there will be a day of judgment after the First Resurrection takes place. It will explain what the Bible means when it speaks of the three distinct groups of people who will occupy the earth. The first group is referred to as the "Firstlings", the "Kings and Priests", the "Overcomers", and "the Bride of Christ". The second group is called the "Lambs", and the third group is called the "Goats".

This book will describe the fate of each group and explain why this world now operates on the physics of opposites, while the new world, because the perfect righteousness of God cannot allow any evil into His new kingdom, will *not* be a world of opposites. God wants all men to learn of Him and accept the offer He provides for them. Scripture however shows us that not all men *will* accept that offer. Therefore I ask the reader to continue through to the end of this book before making any decision and even then to contemplate this information, compare it to scripture, and ponder the consequences of saying no to God's offer. Ask God to help you and to guide you to those things He wants for you, and I am sure that you will be amazed by what you receive. God does not look upon our past or those sins which we may have committed or even the false beliefs we may have held. He looks for an honest and contrite heart which longs for a new beginning and longs to be loved and to give love. Therefore, what God offers is open to everyone.

"And the Spirit,
and the bride say,
Come.
And let him that heareth
say, Come,
and let him that is athirst come.
And whosoever will,
let him take
the water of life freely."

Revelation 22:17

Chapter Two

THE TEN STEPS TO HEAVEN

As mentioned in the opening message of this book, we have all been conditioned to scoff at matters pertaining to the supernatural. Movies, books, and television shows have placed the subject of evil into a category which lacks reality and is for entertainment purposes only. Therefore it becomes a subject that we know little about and cannot discuss with any facts or data. This has not occurred by accident but has been one of the methods used by Satan to accomplish his goal of keeping mankind complacent about his work and his goals. To thwart these efforts, one must be willing to take a step beyond the fear of sounding foolish and look at the prospect of evil, its origins, and its goals, and do so with an open mind. Just as many people avoid discussing politics and religion when an unprofitable debate is likely, so do they avoid discussing the possibility that Satan exists, and that he plays an important role in our personal life. He is not, as cartoons often depict him, a man in a red suit with a dragon tail who holds a pitchfork. He is an angel…a *powerful* angel who, by causing Adam and Eve to sin gained power over mankind. (Matthew 25:41; Luke 10:18; John 8:44, 2 Peter 2:4). Without accepting the existence of Satan as fact, it is difficult to understand why God sent His Son to free man from Satan's power and why He plans a different future world for mankind. But if the reader can move ahead by accepting this information as a premise upon which to build their understanding of God's plan for them, much will be gained spiritually. Further, the decision one makes about their future…. with or without the loving God scripture describes …right or wrong….will become a more educated decision. What is presented in this book can be researched in scripture. God even tells us in scripture that all scripture is given by inspiration of God…for doctrine, reproof, correction and instruction in righteousness. (2Timothy 3:16) God also tells us to test Him. *"....and prove me now herewith, if I will not open you the windows of heaven and pour you out a blessing....."* (Malachi 3:10).

If we sincerely pray for understanding, what cannot be accepted right away may be understood and accepted in the future as God manifests Himself in one's life. However, once Christ returns to earth for the First Resurrection, and grace is removed, *there is no further time to have our sins forgiven.*

This book will attempt to simplify the tenets of God's plan for mankind by creating ten basic steps for that process. The first four of these "ten steps to heaven" is simply a matter of learning what the Bible teaches us about our Heavenly Father, how He views our life here on earth, and what will follow after death. It will explain the nature of man, his downfall and his rise, and his struggle to change his nature from the self serving Adam-like nature to the self sacrificing nature of Christ. This presentation should be viewed with an open mind from beginning to end and carefully considered before any judgment is offered because it describes the incredible love God has for us and how we can gauge *our* life through the eyes of such a perfect love. It is also about how God is working toward the creation of a kingdom which will be forever free of hate and envy, sorrow and pain. In very simple terms, the path to heaven requires every soul who was ever born, conceived or died to understand the ten basic steps about why we are here and to what purpose we are to develop. These ten steps are as follows:

1) Learn of God's plan of salvation
2) Learn why Satan works in our life
3) Acknowledge the stakes in the war between good and evil
4) Learn what God has instituted to allow mankind renewed access to Him
5) Accept these four premises as biblical truths
6) Make a conscious decision to follow God's precepts
7) Desire to develop faith in, and love and thankfulness for God
8) Make use of the sacraments God has provided for us
9) Hate our sins and have true remorse when we commit them.
10) Wage a daily battle to strive to overcome, to follow God's precepts, and to believe

While the first four steps suggest that we gather information about God's plan of salvation and why it was instituted, the next three steps require us to make a decision about that information. We are then required to decide of our own free will whether or not we will move forward, whether or not we can accept what we have learned as truth, and whether or not we desire to apply God's plan to our lives. Thus, the first seven steps to heaven can be accomplished easily, privately and on a personal level. They do *not* require any life changing attitudes or actions, but are to touch our heart with a new outlook about the offer we have been given. Step 8, however, *does* require an action which can only be taken if we complete the first seven steps. It is here where our personal commitment is made. It is at this step where we ask God to make us a part of His family and tell Him that we want to receive the sacraments which will allow us to do so. (Matthew 3:13-17; 28:19-20; Luke 22:17-20; John 6:27; Acts 8:14-17; 1 Corinthians 11:23-26)

These sacraments, as you will learn in the following chapters can only be bestowed by an ambassador of Christ. (2 Corinthians 5:20; 11:2). Steps 9 and 10 tell us what is required for us to fulfill the requirements for receiving the sacraments described in Step number 8. Each of the sacraments is a covenant with God....made *directly* between the soul receiving them and God Himself and must not be taken lightly. They must be requested and revered, and the pre-requisites which God has established for each of them must be understood. Step number 9 requires that we acknowledge our sins and hate them even when we continue to commit them. However, we are also required to have true remorse for having committed those sins, be willing to forgive those who sinned against us, and *strive* to never commit those same sins again. Without meeting these four requirements we will *not* obtain the forgiveness of our sins. Step number 10 recognizes that to follow God when attacked by evil is a *daily* struggle for the children of God, and that we need our faith and we need God to accomplish this. In time we learn that faith is like a muscle because it becomes stronger with use. Without some work of its own, it cannot grow, nor be asked to perform a feat which requires strength. However, faith, unlike a muscle, can and does respond to the heart which longs to follow God and trusts that it can lean on God for help when it falls short. To better understand the first two steps (which are God's plan of salvation and why Satan does what he does), let's begin with an accounting of what occurred in heaven before man was formed. (Mathew 25:41, Luke 10:18, John 8:44 and 2 Peter 2:4).

When God decided to enlarge His heavenly family, he desired that those who would live in His household and reign with Him and His Son were to be kind, loving, long-suffering, honest and loyal. The new kingdom which He planned for these souls would be devoid of all sin and unrighteousness. However, when God created mankind for this purpose, and explained that man would be elevated to a higher position than the angels, jealousy was born in heaven, and a war was waged against God and all of mankind to prevent God from fulfilling His plan. Satan, whose original name was Lucifer, was the highest and most beautiful of all angels, and in his anger, he waged a war with God. He was jealous of Christ and jealous that man was to be elevated "higher" than the position he held in heaven. Satan enticed one third of all the angels in heaven to join his rebellion against God and when he was defeated, he and his followers were thrown to earth. Satan continued his war against God by causing man to sin whereby man lost his access to God. But God, knowing what Satan would do, created the means by which man could return to God. This was through the sacrifice of Christ which paid for our sins. God then offered us the sacraments which erases original sin (Baptism), forgives our daily sins (Holy Communion) and bestows upon us the gift of the Holy Spirit (Holy Sealing) to teach, guide and protect us. Satan however, is fully aware that God will imprison him, and the angels who joined his rebellion, when the plan of salvation is fulfilled and God gains that last soul who will fill His new kingdom. This explains why we are under attack, why we sin, and why we wait. However, the development required to move from the behaviors of a child to becoming a perfect spiritual adult requires a certain amount of time. To develop the qualities which God seeks requires knowledge.... and the application of that knowledge. Knowing that Satan works to prevent man's spiritual development, God has placed into His plan of salvation the sacraments which, through grace, allows us access to Him once again and has given us the free will to choose to employ them....or not. The bottom line is that God chose mankind to become a part of His family, but only if we *freely* desire to do so and are willing to meet the responsibilities attached to that invitation. Psalm 40:8 explains what God hopes will live in the heart of His children: *"I delight to do thy will, O my God, yea, thy law is within my heart"*.

Chapter Three

THE SACRAMENTS

This chapter is mostly about doctrine and therefore requires that the scripture which supports that which follows is provided to the reader so what is written can be authenticated. If one prefers, they can skip over the references to scripture to allow for a quicker flow of information. But the references are there so the reader can come back to the material they wish to verify. The three sacraments which are described below were initiated because the sin of

Adam and Eve separated man from God and thereby, under God's rules of righteousness and having no means of forgiveness, denied all of mankind access to God. Therefore, God provided three sacraments which would allow man to enter into a covenant with Him which would re-open that access through a series of specific requirements. The sacraments hold no power however without first receiving, accepting, and trusting the sacrifice Christ made for our sake so we could be "ransomed" from the captivity of sin. The three sacraments are a covenant or an agreement between God and man and are known as: Holy Baptism, Holy Communion and Holy Sealing.

Holy Baptism is the rebirth by which man can again be linked to God through its covenant. To receive Holy Baptism, man is required to renounce the work of Satan and express the desire to follow God's precepts. It can then erase the claim which Satan has made upon mankind through the sin of Adam and Eve. (John 3:5; 1; Peter 3:21; Matthew

28:19; Matthew 19:14). It is a prerequisite for both the forgiveness of personal sin, and for receiving the Holy Spirit.

Holy Communion is the remembrance of the sacrifice which Christ brought for each of us as a ransom for the sin of man. Its power can cleanse us of our sins provided we have remorse for those sins, *desire* never to commit them again, hate the sins, and forgive those who have sinned against us. (Luke 18:13; 1 Corinthians 7:8-10, Matthew 26:26-28; John 6:53-56). When one takes Holy Communion unworthily it does *not* bring him into fellowship with God or with Christ. (1 Corinthians 11:27-29 and Hebrews 13:10) Partaking of Holy Communion *unworthily* marks the person who does not earnestly desire to overcome his weaknesses and is therefore someone who is irreconcilable and indifferent.

Holy Sealing requires that the first two of the three sacraments mentioned here be previously obtained and through their cleansing and instruction, allows for the administration of the Holy Spirit. The Holy Spirit is the comforter and teacher of the soul and when it indwells man, it provides man with a greater understanding of God's work and protects him from spiritual harm. It is obtained through the laying on of the hands of an ambassador or Apostle of Christ. (Acts 8:14-17; 19:6; 1 Timothy 5:22; 1 Timothy 1:6; Hebrews 6:2, and 2 Corinthians 3:6, 8). It is important to note that one can lose the Holy Spirit through sin, and that one can fall away from the faith without it. (Hebrews 6:4-6)

Scripture tells us that the greatest evil is falling away from the living faith and the greatest sin (which cannot be forgiven), is the sin against the Holy Ghost. Therefore the gift of the Holy Spirit must be guarded and appreciated. (Matthew 12:31-32; Mark 3:28-30; 16:16; and Luke 12:10) Scripture clearly warns that flirting with satanic spirits can allow those spirits to enter the soul of man preventing the Holy Spirit from indwelling that man. That man then becomes a pawn in the hands of Satan. (1 Chronicles 21:1) While these three sacraments can be requested and even administered, once requested those who will arrange for the provision of these sacraments must assess the individuals understanding of what they have asked for. A series of talks or lessons may be initiated to be sure that the individual understands the importance of the vow they will offer to God as they partake of these sacraments. *They will also have to understand the consequences of breaking these vows to God.*

God looks into man's heart and can see the sincerity of that heart. It is therefore not simply a matter of knowing scripture, quoting verses, or even proclaiming one's faith, but a matter of *the relationship* which exists between that person and God. It is therefore important to acknowledge that all relationships require nurturing and to nurture our relationship with God, we need to talk with him.

Prayer is an excellent measure of the depth of our relationship with God, even a prayer in which one stumbles to express themselves can bear the most beautiful fruit when that heart is humble, contrite, and truly in love with God. As our relationship with God deepens, we begin to experience a pious, childlike and personal reverence for God and express complete faith in the promises He has made. This reverence is often noted when one prays and tears fill their heart and the heart of those who hear that prayer. This denotes a special exchange of love and helps us maintain a connection and a close relationship with God. When we pray aloud with our family or with other children of God, we all benefit from the thanksgiving and intercession we hear. Prayer demonstrates a child-like faith, a strong trust and a sincere love. In fact, prayer demonstrates the type of relationship we have with God as it emulates the love and intimacy of our relationships with a beloved spouse or child.

When we pray in the morning, at night and whenever we eat, and we also add those times when we seek God's protection or to say thank you, God knows that we desire to invite Him into every aspect of our lives and seek to support and build the relationship we have with Him. We can learn how to pray from "The Lord's Prayer" which Christ prayed (Matthew 6:9-13), from the prayer Christ offered on our behalf (John 17:24-25), from the prayer Christ offered before He was arrested (Luke 22:42) and from the admonitions scripture provides about not praying vain repetitions and not simply to impress others. (Matthew 6:7). We can also learn how to pray from our ministers and fellow believers.

One of the miracles of our faith is that we are never stagnant. What we may not have understood earlier or that which we initially could not overcome, suddenly becomes that which we *do* understand and that which we *can* overcome. Some efforts take longer than others, but as we look back over a year's time we can recognize the growth in our spiritual life and witness that we have become more of the kind of person God is looking for. We can measure both the tenets of our faith and our personal behavior by applying the "Fruits of the Spirit" to the activities they espouse. Scripture tells us that this comparison is pleasing to God. This demonstrates that as the Holy Spirit becomes a stronger and stronger influence in our lives, we become more Christ-like in nature. Over time we begin to shed the selfish Adam-like nature with which we were born and begin to develop the self sacrificing, loving nature of Christ. We begin to free ourselves of those satanic spirits which work to keep us in a sinful state, and keep us ignorant of many of our sins. As we break free, our faith grows and our nature changes. Scripture tells us that as we walk in the Spirit of God, allowing the Holy Spirit with which we were sealed to live in our heart and to work in our lives, we will practice the fruits of the spirit which are love, joy, peace, longsuffering, gentleness, goodness and faith. (Galatians 5:22)

Chapter Four

WHY DO I SIN?

Satan has a great deal of power over mankind. Scripture clearly tells us that he can make us do as he bids (1 Chronicles 21:1), he can cause illness (Job 2:7), he can take God's word from men's hearts (Mark 4:15), he can produce signs and wonders by which to convince us of a false doctrine (2 Thessalonians 2:9), and that he has many other powers to use against mankind as well. However, the good news is that when we have been sealed with the Holy Spirit we are given the power to recognize, avoid or overcome many of the situations Satan presents. We are given a sort of sixth sense by which we can discern the spirits (fallen angels) belonging to Satan. Nevertheless, Satan's goal and desire is to trap us and make us captive to sin. A perfect example of this is when someone becomes a drug addict or an alcoholic and falls away from God and godly pursuits. However, scripture teaches us how to avoid these traps and even how to break that captivity if it occurs.

But sadly, all men are sinners. The sin of Adam and Eve and the separation from God which this demanded left us with the proclivity to sin. Knowing this, God arranged for the forgiveness of our sin if we seek that forgiveness worthily. Romans 5:12 tells us: *"Wherefore.....for that all have sinned."* And 1 Timothy 2:2-4 tells us *"....that we may lead a quiet and peaceable life in all godliness and honesty. For this is good and acceptable in the sight of God our Savior; Who will have all men to be saved, and to come to the knowledge of the truth."* Through these verses we understand that not one among us is without sin and that each of us must individually find our way to Christ to obtain the forgiveness of our sin. We also learn that it is through the truth of God's words that we can find what we are seeking, and with full and true remorse for our sins, we can find the forgiveness which is required for us to be a part of God's new kingdom through the sacrifice Christ made for us.

Although Adam and Eve's sins made it possible for Satan to separate man from God and gain control of him, God had already instituted into His plan of salvation a way for man to return to God. This, as we mentioned, is through Christ's sacrifice for us and through the three sacraments God provided.

While all sin requires a just payment, the sacrament of Holy Communion is effective because Christ made that payment for each and every one of us through His death. He was the ransom which was paid for our soul. However, we must engage a specific action (Holy Communion) and present a specific hearts attitude (forgiving others, hating our sin, and working not to commit that sin again) to ask for and expect that ransom to cover us.

As we grow in faith, Ephesians 4:14-15, explains, *"That we henceforth be no more children, tossed to and fro, and carried about with every wind of doctrine, by the sleight of men, and cunning craftiness, where they lie in wait to deceive. But speaking the truth in love, may grow up into him in all things, which is the head, even Christ."*

These words show us that God is aware of our status as children who make mistakes, but these words also show us that God expects us to mature and put aside those inclinations and do so by learning what He asks of us, and placing His words into our hearts and into our actions. 1 John 3:8

clearly says, *"He that committeth sin is of the devil; for the devil commiteth sin from the beginning. For this purpose the Son of God was manifested, that he might destroy the works of the devil."*

Additionally, 2 Corinthians 5:17, explains, *"Therefore if any man be in Christ, he is a new creature; old things are passed away; behold, all things are become new."* 2 Corinthians 5: 21 instructs, *"For he hath made him to be sin for us, who knew no sin; that we might be made the righteousness of God in him."*

Without the sacrifice of Christ all men would be bound forever with Satan in the second death of eternal torment and none would have eternal life with God. Through Christ however, grace has been offered to those who will follow Christ through both their belief and the works which that belief inspires. Further, scripture tells us that the requirement to learn of God's words is tantamount. Without knowing these words we cannot know God and without that knowledge we cannot please God. It is not just a matter of faith, but a "doing and working" of our faith which is required and which creates in our hearts the strength and desire to grow into all that God wants for us.

John 14:21 explains, *"He that hath my commandments, and keepeth them, he it is that loveth me....and I will love him, and manifest myself to him....."* John 14:23-24 tells us, *"....if a man love me, he will keep my words, and we will come unto him, and make our abode with him. He that loveth me not keepeth not my sayings; and the word which ye hear is not mine....."*

John 14:26 says, *"But the Comforter, which is the Holy Ghost, whom the Father will send in my name, he shall teach you in all things, and bring all things to your remembrance, whatsoever I have said unto you."*

James 2:17 emphatically states that *"Even so **faith,***

if it hath not works, is dead, being alone." James 2:26 tells us, *"For as the body without the spirit is dead, so faith without works is dead also."*

It follows that if we need works to accompany our faith we cannot *know* what works we need to do without knowing God's instructions about *how* we should work. Works of faith include how we should treat one another, how we should instruct, exhort, and rebuke ourselves, our family, and our neighbors and how we can utilize the sacraments God provides. We also learn that some of these works include prayer, tithing, keeping the Sabbath holy, listening to and learning the word of God and fully understanding and utilizing the protection God offers us. To accomplish these tasks we must understand evil, why we are stalked, and how to fend off temptation. We must also become the teachers of all these truths.

All sin is unacceptable to God. If we acknowledge this and seek forgiveness for *every* sin, and we try, as Christ said to "go and sin no more", we please God. When we study His word and become enlightened by the incredible scope of what true love shows us, we become even more aware of what sin is and how we can change our lives. What was once a sin of no consequence to us soon becomes a sin of great consequence because we have been enlightened by the love we learn through knowing God. Sadly, we are born with the ability to love only selfishly, whereby we seek only *personal* reward. But as we bask under the perfect love of Our Heavenly Father and His Son, we begin to view love in an unselfish light and learn how to serve others and appreciate their service. When we experience the perfect love which Christ and our Heavenly Father so freely give us, we cannot help but want to emulate that love by doing what is pleasing to them. This is a miracle of transformation and it occurs as we shed the selfish love of our Adam-like nature for the perfect love of the Christ-like nature. It creates in our heart and soul a less sinful and more godly nature.

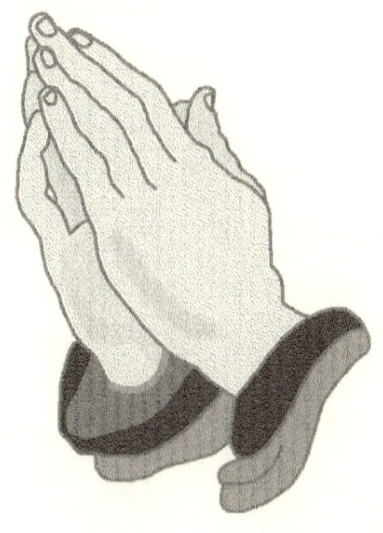

Chapter Five

WHY MUST WE SUFFER HEARTACHE?

As we mentioned earlier, until Satan is bound he will reign on this earth and continue to wield his power. God, fully aware of this, has provided not only the forgiveness of our sins, but also His comfort and His promise to turn all our heartache into a blessing. In many cases the blessing is what we have learned from our experience and what direction our lives take as a result of that experience. God tests us during our times of heartache and tells us that we are being refined for His new kingdom as gold is refined in a fire. It is however, difficult to live through heartbreaking circumstances especially when Satan can cause us to believe that perhaps God does not hear, or desire to answer, our prayers.

When difficulties continue with no end in sight we can become discouraged and may even question our faith or our worthiness to have our prayers heard. We may wonder what we did wrong to deserve what has befallen us. These are normal human reactions, but they are not godly; they come from Satan. In fact, Satan brings us heartache because he wants us discouraged by that heartache and wants us to blame God, feel unworthy of God's help, and question what appears to be God's lack of intervention.

However, God factored this into His plan of salvation and provided us with a way to overcome this difficulty. He offers His comforting presence

(The Holy Spirit) during that struggle and through scripture teaches us what we need to know. Further, our Heavenly Father is both omnipotent and omnipresent which tells us that He is aware of everything at all times. Romans 8:28 tells us, *"And we know that all things work together for good to them that love God, to them who are called according to his purpose."* Thus we are shown that there is a reason why we live through heartache.

When we understand why God allows our struggles, those struggles are easier to bear, and the blessing we can derive from the experience may become evident to us more quickly. Our job is to believe that a blessing *will* come, and to believe that good things *will* result from what transpires in our heart as we go through our difficult circumstances. In fact, when we know what scripture tells us about this phenomena we easily place our faith in God's help and wisdom. Just as God went with Shadrach, Meshach and Abednego into the furnace (Daniel 3:20), and with Daniel into the den of lions (Daniel

6:6), and with David when he faced Goliath (1 Samuel 17:49), He goes with us.

Our heartache is also the time when we can demonstrate our trust in and loyalty to God. When we trust in His decisions He will strengthen us while we suffer heartache. However, when we are not aware that it is *Satan* who brings our heartache and that God creates a blessing from it, and thus we do not trust God, our heartache is more difficult to bear, and the blessing harder to recognize. *We often remain in that heartache longer than necessary had we understood what we needed to do.*

When we have an intimate relationship with our Heavenly Father, His words touch a chord in our heart which allows us to internalize His loving, gentle nature. With this in our heart and mind we begin to change our inner nature and we develop a trust in God which grows stronger over time. We muster our strength to wait patiently for our circumstances to change and learn to dismiss our anger, fear, anxiety, and doubt. Most importantly, we can thank God for our circumstances because we know that they bring valuable changes to our heart to create in us one who *can* become a part of the family God is grooming for His new kingdom. When we understand *why* we suffer and what the outcome will be, we endure more easily. Fellowship with other believers can help us. If we share our worries and our triumphs with one another and bear one another's burdens we will uplift one another in times of sorrow. We can pray for one another, remind one another of the various verses in scripture which may pertain to our circumstance, bask in the promise that God never leaves us, and provide love, forgiveness and encouragement to one another. These are some of the attributes of love which God looks for in those He wants to inhabit His new kingdom. All hate, envy, anger and vengeance will be bound and cannot enter God's kingdom.

Our Heavenly Father is loyal to us and expects us to be loyal to Him and to one another, especially during difficult circumstances. God loves us. He teaches us *through* the difficulties Satan brings into our lives. He works miracles from what we experience and is pleased when we use them to help others deal with their difficulties. He wants us to grow from children into those who are mature in faith, and this can only be accomplished if we ourselves develop in love and understanding, compassion and strength. We will bring those qualities *with us* as we work side by side with Christ in the new kingdom. However, most of us have at one time or another asked the question, "Why, God, why?", or perhaps "How long do I have to suffer?" Asking these questions can make us feel guilty and believe that we have failed God by not trusting Him or not believing that what we go through is known by Him. Many have felt this same despair and asked these same questions even knowing that their troubles are not instigated by God but by Satan.

We must remember that Satan's power is so all-encompassing that he not only challenged God but also engages in a war with God which he believes he can win. We tend to forget that Satan would never have begun such an effort if he thought that he would lose. That alone should tell us that Satan is a formidable enemy. Further, if we have not had our share of heartache, we must examine our heart to see *why* Satan leaves us alone. God wants us to examine our motives and actions on a regular basis so we can always adjust what still needs adjusting and be sure that love is always our motivator. Satan may have us where he wants us if we never suffer heartache.

Our Heavenly Father has a far greater power than the power of evil and will win the spiritual war in which we are all engaged. His plan of salvation will prevail despite Satan's efforts. Nevertheless, banning all evil for all eternity under His own rule of righteousness requires God to *temporarily* allow Satan his challenge. We therefore, must acknowledge that *we* do not have a greater power than Satan, *nor* do we have an equal power, and are thus pawns in Satan's hands *except* for God's protection and direction. The Biblical story of Job demonstrates how Satan can do with us as he pleases……. *except* for the limits placed on Satan's power by God. This story also demonstrates that what Satan is allowed to do cannot destroy those who seek and love God. Therefore, when we tire, when we become discouraged and when we question God, He understands. He has witnessed…and allowed….what we must go through. He uses our sorrow to our benefit and *always* brings from it a blessing.

God Himself suffered greatly as He witnessed the pain and sorrow which Christ endured and He remembers that even Christ said in His agony, *"Let this cup pass from me."* Our Heavenly Father suffers when we suffer as well. Christ understood that He must endure His pain and suffering for a greater purpose. Despite His human fear, He held firm to His purpose and said to God, *"Not My will, but Thy will be done"*. When we follow Christ's example and demonstrate our loyalty to and trust in God during difficult circumstances, it is not the questions we ask or the agony or anxiety we feel, or even the weakness and failure we exhibit which

God counts, but the *final* submission to His will that He looks for, and which will produce the miracle of transformation in our soul.

We should marvel at how profound it is that God turns evil into good so that *all* things work for the good of those who love the Lord. And, we should marvel at how much this can comfort us as we go through our trials and tribulations.

God is working a great miracle for us in that He is preparing a world, under the rule of His righteousness, which will ban all evil. This means that we will *never* know sorrow or pain in that new world. Scripture tells us that love will reign in that new world. Therefore whatever sorrows we must experience here on earth is worth what we will gain for all eternity. Revelation 1:3 tells us: *"Blessed is he that readeth, and they that hear the words of this prophecy, and keep those things which are written therein: for the time is at hand."*

Scripture also tells us that understanding these truths is a gift from God and often refers to these precepts as a mystery. In fact, Ephesians 1:8-9 explains: *"Wherein he hath abounded toward us in all wisdom and prudence; having made known unto us the mystery of his will....."* And Revelation 3:20-21 tells us: *"Behold, I stand at the door, and knock: if any man hear my voice, and open the door, I will come in to him, and will sup with him, and he with me. To him that overcometh will I grant to sit with me in my throne, even as I also overcame and am set down with my Father in his throne."* This is such a beautiful offer.

And.....we also have the incredible promise of Revelation 2:10 which tells us: *"Fear none of those things which thou shalt suffer...."*

Then Revelation 21:4 comforts us with the words: *"And God shall wipe away all tears from their eyes; and there shall be no more death, neither sorrow, nor crying, neither shall there be any more pain...."*

Chapter Six

WHAT WILL HAPPEN TO SATAN?

As we read scripture, the beautiful plan which begins and ends with God's desire for the future of mankind is unveiled. God, knowing that man would sin, arranged for him to learn of good and evil so he would have the opportunity to freely choose good, to repent of all evil, to seek the forgiveness of his sin and to seek a life with God. Scripture teaches us that God longs to fill His kingdom with souls who will truly love one another, and love His Son and Him above all things. Matthew 22:37-39 says, *"Jesus said unto him, Thou shalt love the Lord thy God with all thy heart, and with all thy soul, and with all thy mind. This is the first and great commandment. And the second is like unto it, Thou shalt love thy neighbor as thyself."*

God wants these souls to understand the value of love, trust, and loyalty, and to practice these attributes voluntarily. (John 14:23) As previously mentioned, God began His plan of salvation by creating the earth in its limited universe. Then He created Adam and Eve to live happily in the Garden of Eden, walking and talking with Him. But the angel Lucifer, later known as Satan, rebelled against God because he was jealous of Christ, and of the new being, man, whom God planned to elevate above the angels. (Isaiah 14:12-15) As a result of his rebellion, Satan was thrown to earth with the angels (Revelation 12:9) who also rebelled against

God by following Satan and thereby also disobeyed God. These numbered one-third of all the angels. Satan understands that when God's plan is completed, and God has obtained the number of faithful loving souls He longs for, Satan will be thrown into Hell for what he has done and with him, all the fallen angels. *All* evil will be forever bound. Therefore, to prevent God's plan from moving forward and thus forestall his own destruction, Satan destroyed God's relationship of trust and loyalty with Adam and Eve by enticing them to sin through disobedience. Satan knew that sin would automatically separate man from God because of the rule of God's perfect righteousness. Thus, God then had to banish Adam and Eve as he had banished Satan. (Genesis 3:1 and Genesis 3:23) But God, knowing what Satan would do, provided a way for Adam and Eve, and the generations to follow, to escape the captivity of Satan through the forgiveness of sin....and return to God. To accomplish this goal and pay the ransom for the sin of man, Christ offered Himself as the perfect sacrifice by which the sins of man could be forgiven. (John 1:29) At every turn, Satan interfered with God's plan, trying to destroy those who tried to follow God, because when God developed the number of souls He desires for His new creation, Satan will be bound forever. Thus Satan and his fallen angels, knowing God's plan, fight for their life when trying to draw us into sin.

God's plan is so encompassing that it also provides for those who died in sin both before and after Christ brought His sacrifice for them, by creating a means of testimony in eternity while grace is still available on earth. Christ entered hell after His death to give testimony of His triumph to those who had died in their sins before He could bring His perfect sacrifice. (Luke 24:46) He told them that now they too could find forgiveness. (1 Timothy 2:4). Therefore we are asked to pray for those in eternity who require forgiveness. However, a specific amount of time has been allotted in God's plan of salvation for His chosen ones, living and dead, to be made ready. (Acts 1:6-7) When that time is up, God will send His Son back to earth for the First Resurrection (Revelation 20:5) when He will take to heaven both those from eternity who have obtained forgiveness and those alive who have remained faithful. (2 Peter 3:10) When they are gone, grace will also be gone, and the final destruction of the end times will begin on the earth where, among other things, one-third of all the people on earth will die. When the destruction ends, God will send His Son back to earth with those He had taken at the First Resurrection. They will have celestial (perfect) bodies, and will reign with Christ for one thousand years to bring testimony to everyone living or dead who was not taken in the First Resurrection. Satan will be bound during these thousand years, therefore all of mankind will accept Christ's testimony. However, although God wants all men to be saved, and offers salvation to those souls who remained on earth after the First Resurrection, these souls who accept God's offer and remain faithful after being tested will not be a part of God's family, but *can* become a part of God's community. Scripture refers to this group as the "lambs". After accepting God's offer during the thousand years of peace, they will be tested when Satan will be loosed again for a little. Thus those who have accepted God in this time period can be tried. (Revelation 20:7) Satan will wreak havoc on those not firm in their faith and many will lose their newfound faith. (Revelation 20:2) The completion of God's plan will take place when the Day of Judgment is instituted when everyone, except those taken by Christ for The First Resurrection, will be judged. Some, who the Bible calls the "goats", along with Satan and his fallen angels, will be cast into the lake of fire and brimstone and tormented day and night forever, (Revelation 20:10 and 15) while others, called the "lambs", will become of part of God's new community. But those who are taken for the First Resurrection will continue to *reign* with Christ in the new kingdom as a part of God's family. They will never have to be judged because their sins were forgiven, and entirely wiped away by God. Scripture tells us that there are a specific number of souls God wants for this special position. 2 Esdras 2:40-41 in the Apocrypha tells us: *"Receive they number O Sion, and embrace those of thine that are clothed in white which have fulfilled the law of the Lord. The number of thy children whom thou longest for, is fulfilled: beseech the Lord that thy people, which have been called from the beginning, may be hallowed."* Our desire is to work toward the completion of God's work here on earth, labor in faith, love, and charity to make ourselves worthy to be a child of God. We work to learn God's words, put on the armour of God, seek forgiveness, strive to be an overcomer, and wait patiently for the completion of God's plan of salvation and the return of His Son.

Love is the absence of hate, envy, jealousy and revenge and if any of these things enter into a doctrine or a way of life, they are not from God but are from Satan. Proverbs 6:16-23 tells us: *"These....the Lord doth hate.....a proud look, a lying tongue, and hands that shed innocent blood. An heart that deviseth wicked imaginations, feet that be swift in running to mischief, a false witness that speaketh lies, and he that soweth discord among brethren. My son, keep thy father's commandment, and forsake not the law of thy mother; Bind them continually in thine heart, and tie them around your neck. When thou goest, it shall lead thee; when thou sleepest, it shall keep thee; and when thou awakes, it shall talk with thee. For the commandment is a lamp; and the law is light; and reproofs of instruction are the way of life."*

We carry the hope in our hearts that soon God will find the last soul and will send Christ to take us with Him. We also do our best to bring testimony of God's plan to others so we can help in the work to find that last soul God longs for. Romans 8:25 tells us, *"But if we hope for that we see not, then do we with patience wait for it."*

Chapter Seven

CAN LIFE AFTER DEATH BE PROVEN?

Scripture provides us with a great deal of information about life after death. Isaiah 5:14-15 addresses hell and says, *"Therefore hell hath enlarged herself, and opened her mouth without measure: and their glory, and their multitude, and their pomp, and he that rejoiceth, shall descend into it. And the mean man shall be brought down, and the mighty man shall be humbled, and the eyes of the lofty shall be humbled".* These verses tell us that those who were pompous, mean, or mighty will enter hell and because there would be so many, hell would have to be enlarged to accommodate them. Isaiah 14:9 also addresses hell saying, *"Hell from beneath is moved for thee to meet thee at thy coming: it stirreth up the dead for thee, even all the chief ones of the earth .. .. "* Isaiah 14:15 warns:*"Yet thou shalt be brought down to hell, to the sides of the pit."* Matthew 10:28 comforts believers with the words, *"And fear not them which kill the body, but are not able to kill the soul: but rather fear him which is able to destroy both soul and body in hell. . . ."* And John 11:25 provides the reassuring words, *"...he that believeth in Me, though he were dead, yet he shall live."* When Jesus received word that his friend Lazarus had died, He was with his disciples a far way from Bethany where Lazarus had lived and died. (John 11:14) Jesus journeyed the long distance to Bethany and arrived when Lazarus had been dead for four days. As Jesus approached Bethany, Martha came to meet Him, terribly distraught over her brother's death. Jesus went with her to the grave and there He prayed. Jesus twice called Lazarus by name and Lazarus rose from death back to life and through this miracle Jesus demonstrated His power over life and death, not only here on earth, but also after we enter into death. There are many areas of scripture which tell us that where the soul goes after death is an active place. For example, 1 Peter 4:6 says, "*. . . for this cause was the gospel preached also, to them that are dead, that they might be judged according to men in the flesh, but live according to God in the spirit.*" Scripture teaches that when Christ died, he brought the testimony of his sacrifice and the grace He offered to those in all realms of hell before ascending to heaven. Ephesians 4:8-10 explains: *Wherefore he saith, When he ascended up on high, he led captivity captive, and gave gifts unto men. (Now that he ascended, what is it but that he also descended first into the lower parts of the earth? He that descended is the same also that ascended up far above all heavens, that he might fill all things.)*" 1

Peter 3:18-20, *For Christ also hath once suffered for sins, the just for the unjust, that he might bring us to God, being put to death in the flesh, but quickened by the Spirit: By which also He went and preached unto the spirits in prison; Which sometime were disobedient, when once the longsuffering of God waited in the days of Noah . ."* And in John 8:56: *"Your father Abraham rejoiced to see my day: and he saw it, and was glad."* John 5:25, *"Verily, verily, I say unto you, The hour is coming, and now is, when the dead shall hear the voice of the Son of God: and they that shall hear shall live."* But the most telling story in scripture can be found in Luke 16: 19-31: *"There was a certain rich man, which was clothed in purple and fine linen, and fared sumptuously every day: And there was a certain beggar named Lazarus, which was laid at his gate, full of sores, And desiring to be fed with the crumbs which fell from the rich man's table: moreover the dogs came and licked his sores. And it came to pass, that the beggar died, and was carried by the angels into Abraham's bosom: the rich man also*

died, and was buried; And in hell he lift up his
eyes, being in torments, and seeth Abraham afar off,
and Lazarus in his bosom. And he cried and said,
Father Abraham, have mercy on me, and send
Lazarus, that he may dip the tip of his finger in
water, and cool my tongue; for I am tormented in
this flame. But Abraham said, Son, remember that
thou in thy lifetime receivedst thy good things, and
likewise Lazarus evil things: but now he is
comforted, and thou art tormented. And beside all
this, between us and you there is a great gulf fixed:
so that they which would pass from hence to you
cannot; neither can they pass to us, that would
come from thence. Then he said, I pray thee
therefore, father, that thou wouldest send him to my
father's house: For I have five brethren; that he
may testify unto them, lest they also come into this
place of torment. Abraham saith unto him, They
have Moses and the prophets; let them hear them.
And he said, Nay, father Abraham: but if one went
unto them from the dead, they will repent. And he
said unto him, If they hear not Moses and the

prophets, neither will they be persuaded, though one rose from the dead." From these verses we can deduce that when Christ died he descended into hell to bring his testimony of grace to all souls. If everyone in the prison of hell were beyond help, He would not have gone to them to offer them salvation. In Noah's day, God brought the flood to stop the spread of sin. Christ had not yet appeared, so sin could not yet be forgiven. God saved only the few faithful souls in Noah's family and destroyed all others not only to stop the growth of sin but to preserve the line from which Christ would come. But when God saw the destruction and the multitudes of sinners who entered Hades, He made a covenant not to destroy mankind again until the end times. Thus sin grew unfettered until Christ came to pay the price of man's redemption by sacrificing His life. Before He provided this sacrifice, there was no grace available. Only strict and perfect adherence to the Law of Moses could redeem man. Thus, because scripture tells us that all men sin, unless Christ offered salvation to those who had lived under the Law of Moses almost none of the souls from this era could be saved. This would include the entire 5,000 years during which mankind lived before Christ appeared and made His sacrifice. Scripture indicates that Christ's sacrifice was for *all* who had ever been conceived, born or died and tells us that when Christ died on the cross, He went to the *dead* for three days and then to the Apostles still here on earth *before* ascending to God. His mission was to tell the dead of His sacrifice and offer them salvation. However, just as on earth some accept and others do not, some in hell listened and others did not...and this still holds true today. The parable of the rich man and the beggar which was quoted earlier tells us that Abraham comforted the beggar who died at the gates of the rich man's house. The rich man, who died at the same time, went to Hades where he was tormented and found himself "across a gulf" from Abraham and the beggar Lazarus. This passage in the Gospel of Luke is one of the Bible's most descriptive insights into death and clearly describes two separate realms for the dead. This parable, spoken to the Pharisees, illustrates the chasm in eternity between those who in life pursued God and those who pursued material gain. Under the laws of Moses, this rich man would have to be condemned for all eternity. However, when Christ brought the sacrifice which bridged the gulf between the Law of Moses, and the Law of Love, those who had been condemned by the law, but then accepted Christ, believed and repented.... could obtain grace. God clearly tells us in scripture that He wants *all* men saved and has provided the way for them to do this despite their sins. Thus Christ became the mediator for all of mankind when He gave His life and paid the price for the sin of those who *truly repent and strive to follow His precepts.* John 5:25 says: *("Verily, verily, I say unto you, The hour is coming, and now is, when the dead shall hear the voice of the Son of God; and they that hear shall live.")* and the keywords are: "and now is" indicating that the time is here that the *dead* can hear the words of Christ and "shall hear" which means, "are willing to listen" indicating that not all will listen, believe, and repent. Another verse which supports Christ's testimony to the dead is in the words of Christ's Apostles found in 1Peter 3:19. *"By which also he went and preached unto the spirits in prison."* The word prison refers to those who died under the captivity of Satan because of their sin and thus entered hell. Our prayers of intercession can help those who die in their sins to repent and seek forgiveness through Christ. Grace, through Christ, is the major difference between the Old Testament and the New Testament. To be right with God during the time of the Old Testament, man was required to live by the Law of Moses and, if he didn't, he was automatically condemned. However in the New Testament, Christ came to earth heralding in an era of love, forgiveness, and compassion which bridged *both* eras. Sins could be forgiven through Christ if the heart was repentant and man sought God. God made sure that all men would have the same opportunity whether alive or dead to hear what Christ had done for them and to learn of the gift of redemption offered to them. Understanding these two eras, one of unrelenting laws, the other of love, make us thankful that we live in the era of love. However, God has provided for all men in both eras to be saved *if* they will accept what God offers them. 1Timothy 2:4-6 tells us: *"Who will have all men to be saved, and to come unto the knowledge of the truth. For there is one God, and one Mediator between God and men, the Man Christ Jesus; Who gave Himself a ransom for all, to be testified in due time."* This tells us that all men (*all men to be saved*) will receive testimony at some point in time (*testified in due time*) of the ransom (*ransom for all*) which Christ provided for them. However, many will *not* accept and *not* leave their evil ways and will *not* be found worthy. While every person living or dead will eventually receive testimony, not everyone will accept the offer of salvation and follow God's precepts. The rules of righteousness for the new heaven will require that these souls be thrown into the Lake of Fire with Satan for all eternity.

Chapter Eight

WHAT ARE THE END TIMES?

Many agree that the times in which we live are the end times of which the Bible speaks. Despite this awareness few rush to assess their spiritual condition. Caught in the harried pace of life and too busy to give God what they should, many, even some believers, may lose their soul salvation. The Bible describes the conditions of our earth when Christ will return and predicts that we will be so engaged in our daily activities that we will be unprepared when the moment arrives. Matthew 25:40-42 tells us *"Then shall two be in the field; the one shall be taken, and the other left. Two women shall be grinding at the mill, the one shall be taken, and the other left. Watch therefore; for ye know not what hour your Lord doth come."* These verses indicate that only half of those who are faithful will be ready. Matthew 25:10-13 tells us: *"....they that were ready went in with him.....and the door was shut. Afterward came also the other virgins, saying, Lord, Lord, open to us. But he answered and said, Verily I say unto you, I know ye not. Watch therefore for you know neither the day nor the hour wherein the Son of man cometh."* As we read these parables and the words of the Apostles, we learn that though many are called, few will be chosen and that no one knows the exact time when Christ will return. Matthew 24:36 tells us, *"But of that day and hour knoweth no man...but my Father only."* We also read that those who have spurned God's invitation and are not a part of the First

Resurrection, will be in great agony. Matthew 22:12-13 says, *"....how camest thou in hither not having a wedding garment?.....Bind him hand and foot, and take him away, and cast him into outer darkness; there shall be weeping and gnashing of teeth."* Scripture also tells us about the signs we will see as we approach the end times. Matthew 24:4-12,24 tells us, *"....wars, rumours of wars, famine, pestilences, earthquakes in diverse places, hatred toward Christians, betrayal, hatred, false prophets with signs and wonders, iniquity, no love."* Mark 13:12, 22 tells us, *"...brother shall betray the brother....father the son....children shall rise up against their parents....false Christ's and prophets...show signs and wonders".* Luke 21: 25 explains, *"And there shall be signs in the sun, and in the moon, and in the stars....the sea and the waves roaring....Men's hearts failing them for fear...."* And 2 Timothy 3:1-7 tells us, *"...in the last days perilous times shall come. For men shall be lovers of their own selves, covetous, boasters, proud, blasphemers, disobedient to parents, unthankful, unholy. Without natural affection, trucebreakers, false accusers, incontinent, fierce, despisers of those that are good. Traitors, heady, high minded, lovers of pleasures more than lovers of God; Having a form of godliness but denying the power thereof....ever learning, and never able to come to the knowledge of the truth."* 2 Esdras 16:24 from the Apocrypha adds: *"At that time shall friends fight one against another..."* We are also told what Christ will find when He returns. 1 Thessalonians 4:16 tells us, *"For the Lord himself shall descend from heaven with a shout....then we....shall be caught up....to meet the Lord in the air....."* 1 Thessalonians 5:2 warns: *"For yourselves know perfectly that the day of the Lord so cometh as a thief in the night."* Luke 14:16-17, 24 explains, *"...a certain man made a great supper, and bade many......for all things are now ready.........For I say unto you, That none of those men which were bidden shall taste of my supper."* 2 Peter 3:10, 14 tells us, *"But the day of the Lord will come as a thief in the night.....Wherefore, beloved, seeing that ye look for such things, be diligent that ye may be found of him in peace, without spot, and blameless."* The wedding feast will take place for three and one half years while the horrors of evil work upon the earth to fulfill the prophecies of the end times. Afterward Christ and those He took at the First Resurrection will return to earth to bring testimony to all who had spurned His teachings. Satan will be bound during this testimony and then loosed for a little while to test those who accepted Christ's message. After this, Satan will be bound forever. Revelation 20:1-2 tells us, *"And I saw an angel come down from heaven, having a key to the bottomless pit and a great chain in his hand. And he laid hold on the dragon, that old serpent, which is the Devil, and Satan, and bound him a thousand years. And cast him into the bottomless pit, and shut him up, and set a seal on him, that he should deceive the nations no more....."* Those who choose evil over good will join Satan's final fate. Revelation 21:6 tells us, *"And he said unto me, It is done.....He that overcometh shall inherit.....But the....unbelieving, and the abominable...and all liars, shall have their part in the lake which burneth with fire.....*" Acts 20:29 warns, "*For I know this, that after my departing shall grievous wolves enter in among you, not sparing the flock.*" And Revelation 9:6 tells us, "*And in those days shall men seek death and shall not find it, and shall desire to die, and death shall flee from them.*" Matthew 24:21-22 warns, "*For then shall be great tribulation, such as was not since the beginning of the world to this time, no, nor ever shall be. And except those days should be shortened, there should no flesh be saved: but for the elect's sake those days shall be shortened.*" While there may be very little time before we are caught up in the terrors predicted by scripture, we need to look carefully at our lives, and make the necessary corrections. Christ has taught us to love our enemies, do good to them that hate us, bless those who curse us, pray for those who despitefully use us, do to others as you would have them do to us, be merciful, judge not, condemn not, forgive,

give, and rejoice in the Lord. (Luke 6). He has taught us to avoid adultery, fornication, theft, murder, deceit, covetousness, wickedness, lasciviousness, blasphemy, foolishness, and pride and to be meek and kind, loving and faithful. We are told to prepare ourselves as a Bride prepares for a wedding. If we fail to do this and have not developed as He has requested, when we want to go with Christ at the First Resurrection, we will be rejected. But for those who *are* prepared, God tells us not to fear those days. He tells us to be courageous. Psalm 27:14 says: *"Wait on the Lord: be of good courage...."* Psalm 31:24 says, *"Be of good courage, and he shall strengthen your heart...."* Isaiah 12:2 tells us, *"Behold, God is my salvation; I will trust and not be afraid...."* 2 Chronicles 19:11 states, *".....Deal courageously, and the Lord shall be with the good."* Revelation 2:10 tells us: *"Fear none of those things which thou shalt suffer...."* And Luke 12:32, *"Fear not, little flock; For it is your Father's good pleasure to give you the kingdom."* And John 14:27, *"......Let not your heart be troubled, neither let it be afraid."* However, we have also been warned that if we are *not* prepared we cannot expect to be part of the First Resurrection. The parable of the five wise and five foolish virgins clearly demonstrates that for half of those who proclaim themselves ready, the door to salvation will not open to them as we read in Matthew 25:11-12: *".......Lord, Lord, open up to us. But he answered and said, Verily I say unto you, 'I know you not."* In the end, those who remained faithful will experience God's wonderful promise as revealed in Revelation 21: 4: *"And God shall wipe away all tears from their eyes; and there shall be no more death, neither sorrow, nor crying, neither shall there be any more pain....."* Therefore, we should say as Joshua 24:15 says: *"...As for me and my house, we will serve the Lord".* And while we wait we must as John 16:33 and Acts 27:25 tell us: *"Be of good cheer".*

Chapter Nine

WHERE SHOULD I BEGIN?

It's easy to say that by believing in God we have a relationship with God or that by attending church, believing that Christ died for us, and being "good people" we have developed a true relationship with God. While these are commendable, they do not guarantee the kind of relationship God longs to have with us, nor is it enough for us to become the family He seeks. It's a start, but it is not what truly touches the heart of God. An example of a truly intimate relationship can be found in the interaction which exists between a husband and wife who spend time together every evening, believe in their marriage, and share an open, intimate and ongoing exchange with one another. Revelation 3:15–16 warns: *"I know thy works, that thou art neither cold nor hot: I would thou wert cold or hot. So then because thou art lukewarm, and neither cold nor hot, I will spue thee out of my mouth."* To understand these words, let's examine the relationship between a young married couple who are very much in love and discuss how they interact with one another. When we first fall in love, we care so much for the one we love that we devise many ways to demonstrate our love. We may place a note into the briefcase of the one we love as a surprise to be discovered sometime during their hectic day. We might purchase a special treat for them or telephone just to say hello or to provide them with an endearing word. At home we might touch or hug when we move close to our loved one as we pass in a hallway or as we move from room to room or work together in the kitchen. We may complete a chore for them that they have wanted to complete but had not yet found the time to do so. We would communicate intimately with the one we love, share our concerns and ask what their concerns are. We would exchange information about the good and the bad parts of each day, ask advice about how to handle a particular problem and often mention how much we love them. We would discuss the purchases we wish to make and the state of our joint finances. We would act like one entity, entwined in heart and mind and spirit. We would be like-minded. We would appreciate one another and express that appreciation. This is what would keep us close. Every expression of love and endearment would make our hearts soar. Our children would learn from hearing us speak to one another, and from how we respond to people who hurt us, and appreciate those who support us. Our children would learn from the prayers we speak aloud as we pray as a family, and our own hearts would be touched by the prayers we hear from those under our care. We would be a happy family because we are openly expressive with one another. We would not be lukewarm with one another. We would articulate our love for one another and share our triumphs and our burdens with one another. Conversely, would we be happy in a relationship where we are treated with indifference, where the person we love is uncommunicative, acts neither hot nor cold, neither caring nor uncaring. Would we feel loved, important to that person, feel that they cared? Would our love for them become cool and lukewarm? Which type of relationship do we have with God? Do we converse with God as we do with those we love and do we do this many times each day? Do we speak to God of our difficulties and our triumphs as we would with our loved one? Do we trust God and ask His advice as we would with the one with whom we share our temporal life? Do we seek to do little things every day to show God how much we love him as we do with the person we fell in love with? Do we make an effort to learn what pleases God as we did the one with whom we fell in love? If we do not do the things which all good relationships require we haven't yet developed the relationship with God which allows Him full entry into our hearts and minds, into our spirit and our future. And if we haven't yet developed that relationship, we really don't know Him and may be classified as lukewarm toward God. Thus He can rightly say that He knows us not. God wants to develop inhabitants for His new heaven and new earth who will desire to give and show love. How then can He accept those who are not willing to work for the kind of a relationship with Him, which exists between a man and a woman who are deeply in love? How can we love someone to whom we give no time or effort? Only we can answer the question about the relationship we have fostered with God. Each of us must learn to truly love and begin by helping and encouraging one another to understand what a godly relationship entails. Matthew 25:12 warns us that to some God will say, *"I know you not"*. But if we try our best to show our love and act with love we will be equipped to become one of those whom God can bring into His new creation. He appreciates it when we whisper "Thank You" to Him each day. He sees our love when we find ourselves angry yet bite our tongue and then tell Him that we are trying to live as He asks us to live and request His help to do so. He knows that love is the trust with which we describe our worries to Him and ask Him to guide us, trusting that He will. He is touched by the intimacy of the love which allows us to ask Him to bless us and teach us and protect us every day. Love is having the courage to stand firm and fight to retain the values and treasures He has given us. This, along with our repentance, our tithing and effort, our willingness to learn His words and help others, will result in a true relationship of love and trust not only with God but with our brothers and sister in faith. When our hearts are moved, and our eyes fill with thankful tears for the love God gives us, and we strive to be an overcomer, we know that we have finally allowed God to touch our hearts and that we have touched His. That is a relationship with God and that is how to begin.

Chapter Ten

HOW DO I CHOOSE A CHURCH?

One of the most wonderful gifts God has provided for His children is the comfort of others who share their faith. In Galatians 6:2, the Apostle Paul told his congregations: *"Bear ye one another's burdens, and so fulfil the law of Christ"*. And in Galatians 6:6, he said, *"Let him that is taught in the word communicate unto him that teacheth in all good things."* Ephesians 2: 19-22 says: *"Now therefore ye are no more strangers and foreigners, but fellowcitizens with the saints, and of the household of God. And are built upon the foundation of the apostles and prophets, Jesus Christ himself being the chief corner stone; in whom all the building fitly framed together growth unto an holy temple in the Lord; In whom ye also are builded together for an habitation of God through the Spirit."* These words coupled with words in scripture such as fellowship, friend, fellowservant, fellowsoldier, fellowworker, fellowdisciple, and fellowlabourer indicate the bond which God's children should have, and the love which they should share. Fellowship is defined by Webster's dictionary as "companionship", and "the company of equals". This describes the kinship or friendship which God encourages among believers. Because we are so easily influenced by our surroundings, God warns us not to have fellowship with evil but with good... and says in 1 John 1:6-7, *"If we say that we have fellowship with him, and walk in darkness, we lie, and do not the truth: But if we walk in the light, as he is in the light, we have fellowship with one another, and the blood of Jesus*

Christ his Son cleanseth us from all sin." As the Apostles traveled from city to city to bring the gospel to others, God told them to search for someone they knew, someone in their congregation of believers who resided in the city to which they traveled. If they found no one and were to preach to those they wished to convert, God told them that He would choose someone in that city who would help them and believe in their cause. The Apostles enjoyed being with believers, but also being with new converts and those willing to listen, because in such a group they felt safe, comfortable and comforted. God wants no less for us. He knows that when we are tired, or overburdened, or if we feel defeated, those who are close to God and who share our faith will help us and uplift us. Those who love God can pray together, and break bread together as the Apostles did. It is this spiritual comfort which encourages Christians to have fellowship with one another. But it is also because we can find godly advice in this circle as well as any needed admonition. Sometimes we don't recognize when our path is a dangerous one. But in fellowship with other believers, and under the teaching of those who God has appointed as His ambassadors, we learn to recognize this danger and can then heed the words in Ephesians 5:11 which tell us: *"And have no fellowship with the unfruitful works of darkness, but rather reprove them."* And in 1 Corinthians 10:20, *"But I say that the things which the Gentiles sacrifice, they sacrifice to devils, and not to God; and I would not that ye should have fellowship with devils."* It is also comforting to know that when we do make a mistake we are forgiven, encouraged …and still loved and welcome in the circle of believers if we desire to do better in the future. 1 John 1: 3 tells us, *"That which we have seen and heard declare we unto you, that ye also may have fellowship with us: and truly our fellowship is with the Father, and with his Son Jesus Christ."* And in Galatians 1:9, *"God is faithful, by whom ye were called unto the fellowship of his Son Jesus Christ our Lord."* What we seek to understand of scripture can also be revealed to us as we share conversation with believers and as we listen to sermons which the Holy Spirit has inspired. When one is weak in faith others can provide strength, when one lacks understanding others can teach, when one is weary, another will uplift. When our children are exposed to the conversations of our ministers and friends they too are blessed with the growth of their faith. The hand of friendship we receive, and the trust we can obtain through those friendships is precious. The conversations and the role models we are given bring us consolation, comfort, instruction, and love. Philippians 2:1 tells us, *"If there be therefore any consolation in Christ, if any comfort of love, if any fellowship of the Spirit......"* And in Philippians 3:10 we are told, *"That I may know him, and the power of his resurrection, and the fellowship of his sufferings, being made conformable unto his death."* Therefore, we must seek a church which offers us the three sacraments which scripture tells us are necessary to our relationship with God. We must seek a church which does not depart from scripture in its teachings and doctrine. We must choose one where fellowship is encouraged, where unity is paramount, and where its love reaches out to every country and every soul, and encompasses people of every color and every background. We must choose ministers who will *teach* us sound doctrine based in the gospel of Christ. They must be role models who adhere to the same activities of the early Apostles. Acts 2:42 tells us: *"And they continued stedfast in the apostle's doctrine and fellowship, and in breaking of bread, and in prayers."* Further, *we* must pray that God will lead us to where our soul will be fed and where we will develop in faith. Proverbs 3:5-6 tells us: *"Trust in the Lord with all thine heart; and lean not unto thine own understanding. In all thy ways acknowledge him, And he shall direct thy paths".* We want to be a part of God's plan of salvation and experience, as Revelation 21:4 tells us: *"And God shall wipe away all tears from their eyes; and there shall be no more death, neither sorrow, nor crying, neither shall there be any more pain...."*

ABOUT THE AUTHOR

Helen Glowacki is an interior designer, writer, teacher, and motivational speaker. As the host, writer, and producer of the television series "The Contemporary Woman", broadcast by UA Columbia Cablevision, she addressed interior design and the health, relationship, parenting, and life issues of interest to women. She has co-hosted a number of 24-hour telethons featuring celebrity guests, and was a guest co-host for a cable television game show. Her writing credentials include an extensive background as a freelance feature writer and a staff writer for four newspapers, newsletters, marketing manuals, and the designer and editor of two association newsletters. A graduate of William Paterson University, Helen received her Bachelor of Arts degree in Communications, magna cum laude. She also earned an Associate of Science degree, with honors, and is a registered nurse. She has served on the Boards of Directors for two associations and taught interior design for adult school programs.

Helen was listed in *Who's Who of American Women* and *Who's Who of Women Executives,* is a popular speaker at ease with an audience and addresses aspects of interior design, specifically through the application of Divine Proportion, and the work of God and His word through Scripture. Helen also uses the poems she has written, which appear intermittently in her books, to describe God's help in times of difficulty. Her venues have included women's groups, church groups, community service and religious organizations, high schools and colleges, in libraries, on cruise ships, and in large adult and assisted living condominium complexes and as a guest on a radio show, and in theater groups, army camps, and veteran's hospitals.

Profits from the sale of her books go into providing them to various cancer centers, drug rehabilitation centers, and prisons, and to the mission schools of *The Henwood Foundation* in Zambia, Africa. Those who have provided reviews of Helen's books tout her beautiful stories as spiritually uplifting and biblically correct. She also sends many of her books via email to those in countries where they hunger to learn God's word.

Helen's greatest joys are her husband, two children, four grandchildren, and the time she spends in The New Apostolic Church and in fellowship with fellow believers. Her heart's desire is to help others find the love and comforting presence of God through her writing, her interaction with others, her love of research, her remarkable knowledge and interpretation of scripture, and her multiple outreach activities. She has written for Christian magazines and newsletters, Bible study groups, and various other applications. Her joy in teaching others of God's magnificent gifts inspires and strengthens her to work every day to touch as many hearts as possible.

For additional copies of the books by this author visit www.helenglowacki.com

BIBLIOGRAPHY

New Apostolic Church. *The Holy Bible* (King James Version). Canada: Thomas Nelson, Inc., 1972.

New Apostolic Church. *The Holy Bible* (New King James Version). North America: Thomas Nelson Publishers, 1994.

Strong, James. *Strong's Exhaustive Concordance of the Bible.* Abington, Nashville, 1890.

New Revised Standard Version of the Apocrypha, Oxford University Press, Inc., 1991

Description of the book:

WHAT NO ONE IS TELLING YOU ABOUT ADDICTIONS

Written in an easy to read and easy to understand manner, this is one of the most interesting books ever written about addictions. From alcohol and drug addictions to homosexuality, pedophilia and kleptomania, the lusts of these satanic captivities are finally explained through scripture. Few understand spiritual warfare and the spirits which can enter mankind and cause a hunger for that which is displeasing to God. The power of these hungers can be overwhelming and produce such a strong need to feed the invading spirit that those who are captive are often driven to a life of crime and sometimes to their own death. Recognizing what inspires these satanic invasions, what allows them to stay, and what they require to exist, provides a great incentive to seek one's freedom from the slavery they impose. Scripture aptly and clearly describes what is required to create the environment which causes these spirits to leave the soul which they have invaded. This book provides helpful facts about recognizing and overcoming these debilitating inclinations. It also explains the role played by the selfish co-dependency of the enabler and how they mistakenly believe they are helping the addict when in fact they are encouraging them to remain under the captivity of their addiction. "Tough love" and what scripture explains about sin, and a description of generational sin and the tendencies mankind may inherit, and must fight, provides an explanation of why families often find father and son or mother and daughter falling into similar patterns. This non-fiction book will help those seeking to understand the strength and power of an addiction and the personality changes which often accompany addiction. It will help the reader understand why God allows this heartache and what can be done to break its hold on those we love and wish to help. It also provides the supporting scripture which describes and breaks spiritual invasion. Applying scripture to real life situations helps the reader learn about God's plan of Salvation and about the enemy who has waged war with God. Helen's books also address the forgiveness of sin and why God will accept a repentant sinner as a part of the Bride of Christ and what to expect after death. This book, like all the books written by this author is a must read!

Paperback: ISBN 978-1-4507-9075-8

List and Description of Novels

by Helen Glowacki   (Book Size 6 x 9)

When God Broke Grandma's Heart: (208 pages) Rising from sorrow to become a beacon of faith   Grandma struggles in an abusive marriage until God moves her from unequally yoked and broken to the healing of His love and forgiveness. Her granddaughter Sarah learns where to find answers to her problems and carries that legacy to those she loves.   **Paperback: ISBN 978-0-9847-2110-8**

When God Took Grandma Home: (260 pages) About the heartache of drug addiction, of the enemy who destroys children through drugs, why God allows righteous anger, why we should pray for those in eternity and a description an incredible experience of faith for Matt and Sarah about why God allowed such heartache to occur. **Paperback: ISBN 978-0-49847-2111-5**

When Grandma Chased the Spirits: (208 Pages) The magnetism of idolatry, it's invisible power, and the heartache of bearing a child out of wedlock brings debilitating panic attacks to Mary and affects her husband Kevin. When Matt and Sarah tell them about their faith, God engineers a miracle to solve what that they thought impossible to resolve. **Paperback: ISBN 978-0-9847-2112-2**

The Granddaughter and the Monkey Swing: (284 pages) A wedding, a broken engagement, renovating and decorating a home through Divine Proportion, the truth about Halloween, and the gift of role models create a tender story of friendship. Helping through the planning and problems of a wedding culminates in the unveiling of a secret. **Paperback: ISBN 978-0- 9847-2113-9**

Grandma's Little Book of Poetry: The Story of God's Plan of Salvation: (277 pages) This beautiful whimsical story for all ages, begins when Sarah finds a manuscript in Grandma's desk and recognizes the story Grandma read to her and Josh and Caleb when they were children. Angels watch the inhabitants below them struggle to find God. **Paperback: ISBN 978-0-9847-2114-6**

Abiding Faith, Hidden Treasure: (262 pages) Serving in Iraq, Jim loses his faith to see a loving God allow so much heartache. Barbara invites him to dinner where Grandma shows him why creation and evolution co-exist and God's enemy creates the injustices Jim blames on God. Letters from the grave bring an incredible experience of faith. **Paperback: ISBN 978-0-9847-2115-3**

And Then They Asked God: (295 Pages) When Rebecca and Jayden arrive at their college campus they are overwhelmed by betrayal. Losing the values Rebecca once cherished fills her with guilt so monumental that she cannot forgive herself. Chaldeth the evil angel is defeated when God's grace frees Jayden and brings Rebecca's recovery. **Paperback: ISBN 978-0-9847-2116-7**

Caleb's Testimony: (262 pages) Ann and Caleb thought that their faith was strong enough to weather any storm. But when faced with losing everything they'd work so hard for, they recognized their greatest shortcoming. **Paperback: ISBN 978-0-9847-2119-1**

The "Why God Why" Mini-Series

by Helen Glowacki

(Book Size 5 ½ x 8 ½)

***To What Purpose*?**: (126 pages) This first book in the *Why God Why* series answers questions about why we are here, what we need to learn, and what God plans for us. It is an excellent book for testimony and one you will share with others. **Paperback: ISBN 978-1-4507-7580-9**

***Why God, Why?*:** (126 pages) This second book in the *Why God Why* Series describes why we experience heartache, its purpose, and how to face it. It answers questions about God's plan for us and what we need to do to be found worthy. **Paperback: ISBN 978-1-4507-7581-6**

***Why Trust Scripture?*:** (126 pages) This third book in the *Why God, Why* Series addresses the challenges against scripture, who wrote the Bible, the importance of the sacraments, what role Satan plays, and how health and the Bible are related. **Paperback: ISBN 978-1-4507-7582-3**

***What Should I Know about Life after Death and the Coming Tribulation*?:** (126 pages) What occurs following death, what will happen during the tribulation, and what the seven seals could mean to us are explained in this fourth book of the series. **Paperback: ISBN 978-1-4507-7583-0**

***What Does God Want Me to do Right Now*?**: (126 pages) A concise explanation of what God asks of us, how we can live up to His expectations of what is required to become a part of the Bride of Christ, and what God plans for the future with or without us. **Paperback: ISBN 978-1 4507-9076-5**

**Do Our Little Sins Really Count**? (126 pages) Most of us believe that the little sins don't really matter but scripture explains why they do. **Paperback: ISBN 978-0-9847-2117-7**

**What Do Angels Do**? (126 pages) Few understand the hierarchy of angels or their duties, nor that whatever powers the fallen angels had in heaven, they also have on earth. **Paperback: ISBN 978-0-9847-2118-4**

List of Non-Fiction Books

By Helen Glowacki   (Book Size 5 ½ x 8 ½)

Politically Incorrect: The Get Some Gumption Bible Study When Enough is Enough: (298 pages) Fifty timely and controversial issues are examined under the politically correct approach along with a description of what scripture says is the approach that He wants his children to take. **Paperback: ISBN 978-1-4507-9074-1**

Overcoming Depression: How To Be Happy: (258 pages) We all face heartache, and all feel sad from time to time.   But depression lingers and can result from many different causes. It can rob us of hope and destroy our relationship with God.   Thus our Heavenly Father tells us through scripture how we can tap into His blessing and His direction and brings joy out of tribulation. **Paperback: ISBN 978-1-4507-9077-2**

What No One Tells You About Addictions: (216 pages) Discussing the merits of tough love, the selfish co-dependency of the enabler, what scripture tells us about spiritual warfare and invasion, and generational sin, make this book a must read. **Paperback: ISBN 978-1-4507--9075-8**

Book Reviews

Reverend (District Apostle Ret.) Richard C. Freund, President of The New Apostolic Church, USA, Sea Cliff, New York: Magnificent writer, a story which makes the reader become emotionally involved, a joy to read, strong Christian values. *"When God Broke Grandma's Heart",* best seller quality.

Reverend (District Apostle Ret.) Richard C. Freund, President of The New Apostolic Church, USA. Helen's new novel, *"When God Took Grandma Home"* "Delights, brings comfort to those who grieve. Inspires, gives insight into the after-life, masterful portrayal.

Reverend Andrew Muliokela: New Apostolic Church in Alexandria, Virginia, formerly from Zambia Africa: *The Granddaughter and the Monkey Swing* and this series of books are awesome! A journey unlike another, I was reading a great novel, learning about confidence, love and support but also learning Bible verses at the same time! Helen Glowacki teaches through her books and I recommend them 100%. You'll enjoy the journey!

Reverend Frederick Rothe, (Ret. New Apostolic Church, New York) Palm Beach Gardens Congregation, Florida: Spent 48 years serving God and another 30 in the congregation. These books contain an accurate account of what God wants of us and why we suffer. The application of scripture and the people in the stories stand for the principles God wants in all of us.

Reverend Kevin Speranza, New Apostolic Church, Palm Beach Gardens, Florida: *And Then They Asked God* so happy I read this, weaves, documents biblical precepts, addresses political correctness, moral & political corruption, biased teaching, insidious growth of socialism renamed progressivism, self-importance, guilt and its debilitating power. WELL DONE!   Identifies danger, artfully and Biblically addresses them.

Reverend Luke Jansen, Sr. V. P., Medical Connections, Boca Raton, Florida: "To Ms. Glowacki, author of **The Grandma Series**: grateful for your books, refreshing to find a Christian author who sees the *difference* between religion and spirituality AND that the two can and should be used in the same sentence.

Reverend Derryck Beukes, Montana-De Aar Congregation, Northern Cape, South Africa: Dear Helen, I personally often use your articles in my soul care visits, especially where youth are involved. I can assure you that your articles made a difference to my way of thinking, and I am busy encouraging fellow priests to read your works, as they are so factual and insightful! Thank you for your hard work. I thank God for you, and the wisdom He gave you! Please continue with the excellent work.

Deacon Shadreck Wilima, Overspill Congregation, Ndola, Zambia: Your articles prompt realistic examples which New Apostolic Christians need for their everyday living.

Youth Chairperson, Sunday School Teacher, Mulenga Ernest, Lusaka Central Congregation, Lusaka, Zambia: Through your writing I am constantly reminded of what to be aware of. I pray that God keeps you in the hollow of His hand, guards you and guides you to reach your brethren as you do me. Thanks for caring for the souls of many.

Reverend Aurelio   Cerullo, Atripalda Congregation in Campania, Southern Italy: Dear Helen, your books and articles, and social networking bring brothers and sisters the words of our faith and touch the hearts of those who do not know our faith. Our goal is found through the grace of the apostolate and in this sense, the word's from 1 Corinthians 15:58 assumes an important meaning: *"Therefore, my beloved brethren, be steadfast, immovable, always abounding in the work of the Lord, Knowing That your labor is not in vain in* *the Lord"*. Now that I am a minister of God for about a year I too am grateful to our beloved Father in Heaven for having opened the eyes of my soul, for having removed the plugs from my ears of my heart to hear and listen to His will in connection and communion with those who precede us, guided by the light of the Holy Spirit. God's work always evolves and adapts to the times and even via computers, cell phones and smart phones. I Thank God for having been able to know you, you're a very valuable pearl. God bless you richly.

Rev. Fred Krueger, (Ret.) Lutheran Minister 12 yrs and Clinical Social Worker 26 years, Dallas, Texas: "Inspiring, grabs the heart, author headed to the bestseller list, a pleasure to read, masterful. *"When God Took Grandma Home"* filled with insight into God's plan!

NOTE: The articles which are referred to in these reviews are excerpts from Helen Glowacki's non-fiction books. Not shown are reviews by the ministers who oversee *The Henwood Foundation*'s New Apostolic Mission Schools in Zambia and review all reading materials prior to distribution.

Edith Stier, wife of a Ret. District Evangelist, Clifton, New Jersey: *The Grandma Series* helps those in   need, inspirational, heartwarming, ends with a beautiful example of how God explains our pain, renews hope, shows us the way, creates miracles. I love this series.

Patricia Robinson, wife of a Ret. Rector, Indiana 5 star rating: *When God Broke Grandma's Heart*: WONDERFUL INSPIRATIONAL NOVEL, enjoyed this book, well written, Bible references, how to achieve peace of mind and soul .

Rosemarie Schaal, wife of an Ret. Reverend, New York: *Abiding Faith, Hidden Treasure:* Reader develops empathy, feels emotion, hears a battle between scientific and spiritual knowledge. Skillful, detailed, brilliant, vivid, teaches nothing happens that is not planned by Him.

Colette van Loggerenberg, wife of a Minister, Scottsville Congregation of Pietermaritzberg, South Africa: *Grandma's Little Book of Poetry: The Story of God's Plan of Salvation:* This has to be one of the BEST EVER books that I have read....If you ever get the chance to get one of Helen's novels...READ IT. It's like a fairytale but a TRUE fairytale.....Close your eyes and picture this: Grandma with her hair in a bun, glasses perched delicately on her nose, sitting in a rocking chair and her grandchildren sitting on the floor with BIG eyes hanging onto her every word.....but with a twist!!!!! If you have doubts about PRAYER...read this book. I LOVED IT...thank you!

Debbie Espeland, wife of a Rector, Palm Beach Gardens Congregation, Florida: 5 star rating: *When God Took Grandma Home:* HEARTWARMING! This book touched my heart. It is both heartwarming and very spiritual.

Aletta Venter, wife of a Deacon, Scottsville Congregation, Pietermaritzburg, South Africa: *"Grandma's Little Book of Poetry: The Story of God's Plan of Salvation".* What a learning process for me. Oooh I just **love** the way the angels are telling the story, **very original!** When is mankind ever going to learn? The inhabitant's lesson was to learn of good and evil. And they failed miserably each time. The devil has his agenda, and the inhabitants are the target. They call upon God for help, the angels rejoiced. Great....!!!

Aletta Venter, wife of a Deacon, Pietermaritzburg, South Africa: *"Abiding Faith, Hidden Treasure"* is the deepest and most rewarding novel I have ever read, touched my soul, made me cry, author's understanding of God's work is astounding, opens the mysteries

Lisa Mayo, wife of Minister, Palm Beach Gardens Congregation, Florida: Helen's *Why God Why* series of books gave me a new understanding of my faith. They are informative, so enlightening and in-depth, but in a way that is easily understood!!

Tammera Shelton, M.S. Psychology, Odenton, Maryland: I find *"When God Broke Grandma's Heart"* inspirational, beautifully portrays need to let go of negative events and that despite injustice, no pain is for naught.

Robert W. Rothe, USMC 1970-1976, Nevada: 5 star rating: *When God Broke Grandma's Heart:* Outstanding writer, kept me riveted, an angel sent to help through trying days. Thank you for helping me find peace.

Katharina Leipp, Schopfheim, Germany: This is the first time I have ever heard of a female New Apostolic author and I am very impressed by your articles. I have sent your link to my Shepherd and German friends and would like you to consider advertising in our German *Our Family Magazine.*

Claudine Visagie, South Africa: I'm trying to think of a way to introduce Helen's books and articles to others… especially to our youth. They are life changing!

Rabecca Mukuta Mukato, Lusaka, Zambia, Africa: Speaking on behalf of my Dad, District Elder Mukato, your articles are brilliant because they have changed me! Because of your articles my Dad has less headaches!

Robert Henry Parkes, Pietermaritzburg, South Africa: You are gifted with the verses and writings you do and are so inspiring to others. God is really using you as His special servant. You are really a wonderful person and we thank the Lord for you our sister in faith.

Frank Geores, from Port St. Lucie, Florida: *"When Grandma Chased The Spirits:* beautiful spiritual experience, can see caring nature and loving heart of author, eloquently reveals her love for God and search for truth. Worthy of the Star of Bethlehem rating. Thank you for sharing your magnificent gift.

Ben Lodwick, Avid Reader., from Brookfield, Wisconsin: Wow! An eye opener about God's plan of salvation, and why bad things happen to good people. Reminds me of Jim LaHaye and Jerry B. Jenkins "Left Behind Series". MUST READ!"

Dr. Walter Forman From North Palm Beach, Florida: *Grandma's Little Book of Poetry: The Story of God's Plan of Salvation:* a "wonderful book about success and failure in life. All Helen's novels are wonderful, a balm for the soul and an education to the seeker."

Susan Day, From Jupiter, Florida: *Abiding Faith, Hidden Treasure* : I hated to put it down, couldn't wait to pick it up, read all Helen's books, proves every point, shows what to do through God's words. I am 90 and Helen's books have helped me call on God.

Georgette Rothe, From Fort Piece, Florida: *Abiding Faith, Hidden Treasure* was more than I expected; a Biblical course making you re-evaluate your beliefs, enjoyed the journey very much.

Fred D'Alauro, from Palm Beach Shores, Florida: Internet 5 star rating: *When God Took Grandma Home:* Remarkable! Inspirational, moving. Fascinating storyteller with a real message.

Debra Forman, Chester, New York. Internet 5 star rating: *When God Broke Grandma's Heart:* Written from the heart, shares the strong beliefs that shelters us in times of need, courage captivates the reader. Thank you.

Anonymous: Internet 5 star rating: *When God Broke Grandma's Heart:* WHEN LIFE GETS YOU DOWN, PICK THIS BOOK UP, it wrapped its arms around me. A wonderful read. Congratulations on an inspiring work.

A reviewer, a reader in Kentucky: Internet 5 star rating: *When God Broke Grandma's Heart:* Well written, heartwarming, overcoming heartbreak through God, touches your heart. A worthwhile read for all generations.

A reader: Internet 5 star rating: *When God Broke Grandma's Heart:* a must read for all generations. FANTASTIC!

A reviewer Internet 5 star rating: *When God Took Grandma Home:* Moves you, captivating.

A reviewer, a Kentucky reader: Internet 5 star rating: *When God Took Grandma Home:* MUST READ! Touching story of life's tragedies and how lessons learned from these heartbreaking events can turn into blessings.

Characters Found in the Novels
by Helen Glowacki

Grandma: Grandma's life was filled with sibling betrayal and marital abuse. Her love of God, home remedies and famous boxing stance touches the heart.

Sarah: Sarah helps Grandma write her journal, learns about God's plan of salvation and the enemy who wants to harm her. She carries on Grandma's legacy of faith.

Matt: Matt, Sarah's husband, has a rock-like faith but when he loses a loved one, struggles with his anger with God, until he has a miraculous experience of faith.

Paul: Paul is Matt's older brother who earned a Captain's license for a seagoing tugboat. His faith sustains him despite enduring terrible circumstances.

Mary and Kevin: Mary and Kevin become Matt and Sarah's neighbors and friends. Mary's panic attacks end when God brings a miracle they never thought possible.

Elizabeth: Elizabeth adopts Rebecca, loses her husband twelve years later, is confronted with a potentially deadly illness and searches for Rebecca's birth mother.

Rebecca: Rebecca is Elizabeth daughter and Jayden's friend. Her father's death, the illness her mother faces, and a series of challenges at college almost destroy her.

John: John, a deacon, lost his wife to a debilitating disease, becomes Elizabeth's friend, and helps his daughter and grandson through a difficult divorce.

Jayden: Jayden is John's grandson and becomes Rebecca's friend. He has learned that prayer helps solve problems and he and Rebecca begin to share their faith.

Wade and Ruth: Wade is Jim's boss and friend who adopts two children from Iraq. Ruth is Jayden's mother and John's daughter who struggles to let go of the past.

Joshua and Debbie: Joshua, Sarah's younger brother, was demanding and judgmental until Caleb stepped in. Debbie looks to Joshua's family to be her role models.

Caleb and Ann: Caleb is Sarah and Josh's older brother and the family looks to him as they once looked to Grandma. Ann, Caleb's wife harbors a secret sadness.

Barbara and Jim: Barbara, Matt's sister is also Sarah's close friend. Her husband Jim plays devil's advocate in family debates, and matchmaker for his friend Wade.

Heza and Bara: Heza and Bara endured a suicide bomber attack when Bara was one and one half years old and Heza as she was born. They are adopted by Wade.

Chaldeth: Chaldeth is a fallen angel sent to destroy Grandma's family. He plots to bring great heartache to Rebecca and Jayden and their family to break their faith.

Durk: Durk, abused by a cruel father, is a sophomore at the college Rebecca and Jayden attend. He brings harm to Rebecca and Jayden but Jim gives him a second chance.

Professsor T. Nagorra, and Emils, and Dean Peerca: These tenured professors befriend Durk and engage in activities that bring harm to the students and campus.

Professors Doog and Sendnik, and President Legna: These three share a faith in God, a love for their country, and desire to be role models. They help save the campus.

"The Lord is my light

and my salvation;

whom shall I fear?

The Lord is the strength

of my life;

of whom

shall I be afraid?"

Psalm 27:1